OLEG THE SNOW LEOPARD

story by Jean-Claude Brisville / illustrations by Daniele Bour
translated by Anthea Bell

LONDON
VICTOR GOLLANCZ LTD
1978

© Editions Grasset & Fasquelle 1978 / First published in France
by Editions Grasset & Fasquelle in 1978 as *Oleg Le Leopard des
Neiges* / Printed in France / ISBN 0 575 02557 3

It was bitter winter weather in a country in the far North. The cold was intense, the nights seemed endless, but Oleg the Snow Leopard could not rest. The hunters were after him, his shoulder had been mauled by the teeth of a trap, and still he had to run on and on.

One freezing morning he saw dunes on the horizon. He bounded forward, making one last effort. There was a steep slope to climb, and he was very tired.

Through the mist, he saw an empty beach of black sand stretching out ahead. He was caught between the hunters and the sea: this was the end of the road! Oleg raised his noble head and uttered a long, unhappy howl.

Eugenia the Blue Whale, who was asleep out in the bay, opened one eye at the sound, and a shiver of surprise and delight ran down her enormous back. She had never dreamed there could be such a beautiful creature—his body so lean and muscular, his fur so elegantly marked with black stars. Eugenia, who was very fat herself and very self-conscious about it, fell head over heels in love with Oleg. She shot two tall jets of water towards the sky in his honour, but Oleg sprang back, afraid there was some kind of ambush.

He had just enough strength to reach the shelter of a rock, where he lay down to sleep…to sleep for a long, long time.

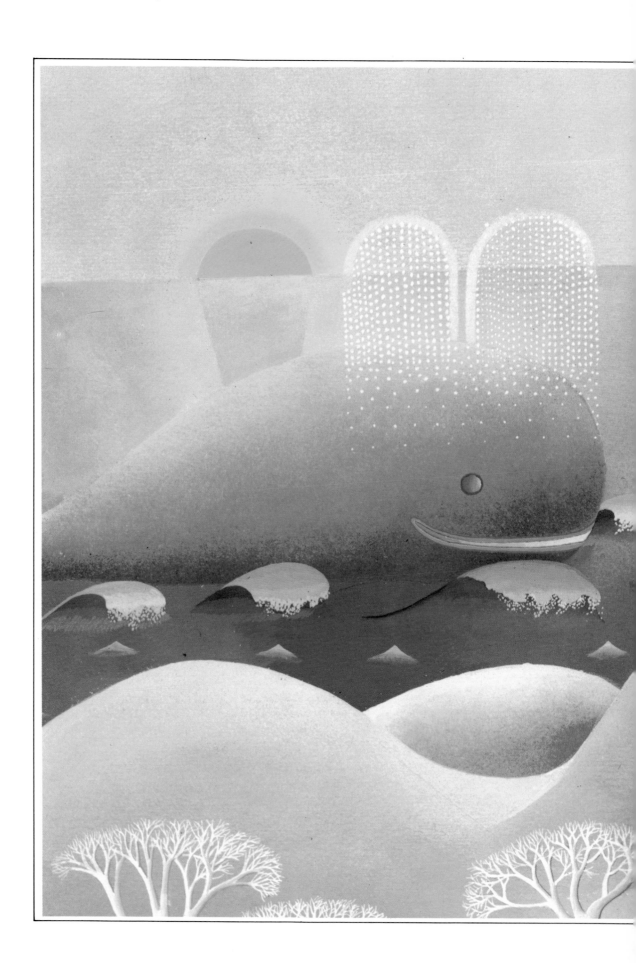

Ivar the Bear strode out of his den, slapping his sides. It was good to breathe the crisp morning air after a nice warm sleep beside his wife Anoushka and their three cubs. "Lovely weather for ducks!" growled Ivar, just as he did every winter morning, and launching himself into a clumsy somersault...he found himself face to face with Oleg. Lying flat on his front, Ivar opened his eyes very wide. "Asleep," he muttered. "Or dead," he added, after a moment's thought. "Unless, of course, he has fainted!" he concluded. Shaking his huge, shaggy head he got up, and went back to his den carrying Oleg in his strong arms.

"Dear me, Ivar, whatever have you brought home now?" cried his wife when she saw his burden.

"A leopard. If he's dead we'll eat him, if he isn't we'll nurse him till he gets better."

And Ivar put the Snow Leopard down on a bed of dry grass. Anoushka came over and felt Oleg's heart with her paw.

"He's alive," she said. "But just look at his poor shoulder! He's lost a lot of blood."

"It's those wretched hunters again!" growled Ivar.

"Yes, they must be on his trail," said Anoushka, sounding worried. "Suppose they follow him here...?"

"We'll fight 'em!" roared Ivar, drumming his paws on his chest. "I'm not scared of humans! No one comes killing animals in my house, not while I'm alive to stop them!"

"Oh dear, don't forget the children..." murmured Anoushka, pointing to their three cubs lying asleep together.

"Yes, you're right," said Ivar, scratching his head. "We must think of the children. Wait a minute...I know! Socrates always has good ideas; he'll tell me what to do."

And he went out of his den, frowning so hard that it made his eyebrows bristle.

Old Socrates the Seal was sitting thinking on his rock above the bay. Socrates was the village mayor, and though he had never known a moment's happiness since the bloodthirsty hunters had killed his young wife Celia the Sea-lion before his very eyes, he was always willing to give anyone who needed it advice. When Ivar had explained the problem, he nodded his gleaming head.

"Well," he said, thinking aloud, "we certainly can't leave the poor thing to those savage human beings—but then again, you mustn't put your children in danger."

"So what are we to do?" asked Ivar.

Just at that moment a strange vehicle came along the path by the sea-shore. Two tall penguins were pulling an exquisite wooden sleigh which was painted red and gold. A beautiful little cat reclined in the sleigh, muffled up in her own silky white fur. Her big green eyes were almond-shaped, she had the prettiest little pink nose, and altogether she looked amazingly elegant.

"I know!" cried the Seal. "Lady Guinevere," he called, raising his harsh old voice. "I'd like a word with you, if I may."

The cat wrinkled up her nose and made a slight spitting sound, to tell her penguins to stop. Socrates and Ivar went up to her very respectfully.

"Isn't she pretty!" said Ivar, admiringly.

"She's said to be a princess…an Eastern princess; Persian, I think," murmured the old Seal. "She came by the Trans-Siberian Railway not so long ago, with any amount of luggage. It's a great honour for our village."

"Where is she living?"

"In a conservatory in the old castle up there. She hired those two," said Socrates, pointing to the Penguins, "so as to have the kind of servants she's used to. Frederick is her butler and Clementine is her lady's maid. Now, keep quiet while I talk to her, please."

So Socrates told Guinevere the Cat about their problem: how could they hide the Snow Leopard without risking the lives of the bear cubs?

"Ah yes…the Snow Leopard!" said Guinevere languidly, half closing her eyes. "A cousin of mine three times removed, I rather think. Have him taken to the castle, and I will look after him."

"But aren't you afraid of humans?" asked the old Seal.

Guinevere yawned; her mouth was like a piece of coral opening.

"Humans just adore me, my dears!" she said, simply. "So that's settled: I'll send my sleigh round this evening to this gentleman's residence." (Ivar swelled with pride.) "Put the poor wounded creature on it, and my servants will take him to the castle."

She nodded graciously to the friends, and told her Penguins to start off again.

"A real lady!" said the Bear warmly, much moved.

"With a heart of gold, too!" the old Seal agreed. "Well, off you go and get the Leopard ready, Ivar. And don't wave your arms about too much, old fellow, you might frighten the Penguins. You don't know your own strength!"

Unfortunately this conversation—or the beginning of it, anyway—had been overheard. Fluster the Hare, hiding behind a bush, had been listening to Ivar and Socrates discussing their plans. Fluster, who was scared to death of practically everything, could hardly believe his ears, long as they were. That great fool of a Bear, sheltering a Leopard with the hunters after him...oh, there was going to be a real killing, and Fluster felt sure no one would escape! There was dreadful danger ahead. How could he prevent it? And at this point a really shocking idea came into his cowardly mind. Once Ivar and Socrates had gone over to meet Guinevere he darted off like an arrow.

He raced on and on until evening before he found what he was looking for: a camp fire out on the steppes. Cautiously, he went up to it and saw two hunters, the Killemoff brothers, warming their hands at the flames. Fluster hesitated for one last moment, and then jumped into the circle of light. One of the hunters reached for his gun, but Fluster got his word in first.

"Oh, brave hunters!" he stammered. "I'd be very poor game for you, I do assure you. Oleg the Snow Leopard is the kind of prey you need...and if you promise to spare my life I'll tell you where to find him."

The Killemoff brothers glanced at one another. Yes, the big animal they had been hunting for so many days and nights was certainly worth more than this hare! Anyway, what was to stop them killing the hare too, once he had led them to Oleg?

"It's a deal!" grunted the elder brother. "Tell us where Oleg is, and you'll be all right. But if you're trying to trick us..."

"Oh, gentlemen, would I even think of such a thing?" cried the hare. "Listen: Oleg is not at all well, and he's staying with Ivar the Bear. It's only a day's journey north if you travel fast. Just follow me!"

"Very well; we leave at dawn tomorrow, and try to lead us straight to the place. You can sleep here overnight."

Fluster humbly lay down by the fire, and tried to forget his own treachery in sleep.

At that very moment Oleg was on his way to Guinevere's conservatory in her sleigh. The Penguins were pulling it and Ivar was pushing it. Oleg had recovered consciousness, and his shoulder did not hurt so much now, thanks to Anoushka's loving care. Ivar and the Penguins put him on an old velvet sofa beside Guinevere, who had to move up a little to make room for him, and then they went away. The Cat and the Leopard were left alone in the dusk. The flames of a wood fire lit the conservatory dimly.

"A cup of tea?" asked Guinevere politely. Since Oleg was too surprised to reply, she went on, "China or Ceylon?"

"No thanks…thank you all the same!" stammered the Leopard. "I'm…I'm not used to it, you see, not at this time of day."

"Just as you please! Make yourself at home."

"You're so kind—I can't tell you how much I appreciate it." replied Oleg.

"Well, big game like us…we should stick together, you know," said the Persian cat. She bared her teeth and spat lazily, showing her sharp incisors, to give more weight to this remark.

Rather embarrassed, Oleg coughed. "Yes, I suppose you could say we were related that way," he said in an undertone.

"And why are the humans after you?" asked Guinevere, curling up into a ball on the sofa.

"For my skin," said Oleg, gloomily. "They want me dead. Have you had anything to do with humans before?"

"Oh, dear me, yes—frequently! I've known them argue with each other over the honour of my company, and some of them have really loved me dearly. But I got a little tired of all that petting, so I decided to take a holiday. I lead a very quiet life here, but I dare say I needed to go back to Nature, you know. And what about you, my dear cousin?"

"I have to keep running if I don't want to end up dead or in a zoo."

"An outlaw…" sighed the Persian cat.

"That's the trouble with being a snow leopard."

They talked all night by the light of the glowing embers. In the morning, after a breakfast of good red meat, Oleg felt better and decided he must leave.

"Come back any time you like!" Guinevere told him at the door. "You'll always be welcome here." The Snow Leopard was so moved he could only kiss her paw.

At the same time, or thereabouts, Socrates, who had gone to sleep nice and dry on top of his rock, suddenly found himself up to the eyebrows in water. Sneezing, he opened his eyes and glared. Eugenia the Blue Whale surfaced beside him, heavily.

"For goodness' sake!" he grunted. "You only have to move and it's like Noah's Flood!"

"Sorry, Socrates," sighed Eugenia, "but I'm so sad, you see. I just can't forget that Snow Leopard. He was so handsome!"

"In love, are you?" asked the old Seal, sarcastically.

"Yes, I really think I am," Eugenia confessed with a blush.

"Dear me, Eugenia!" said Socrates. "Surely you realize this can't come to anything?"

"I love him all the same," said Eugenia defiantly. "Anyway, that kind of thing isn't so important these days. It doesn't really matter if you don't belong to the same race."

Socrates raised his kind, wide eyes to the heavens. Honestly, he wondered, how dim could a Blue Whale get? He tried to make her see reason, but it was no use.

While Ivar was out for his usual morning run, Anoushka was busy getting the cubs up and washed. The Killemoff brothers were pointing their guns at her before she even realized the danger. "Oh, Ivar—they'll kill your children!" thought the poor mother, forgetting that they would kill her too. But at that moment a fearsome howl froze the hunters' fingers on their triggers, turning the blood in their veins to ice. They could not help looking behind them—and there they saw Oleg, glaring at them with his luminous eyes, all his muscles flexed, his whiskers nearly touching them. The terrified Killemoff brothers forgot all about their guns; they turned and ran for it. Fluster, trembling all over and flat on his front in a copse, watched them go. Anoushka rushed up to Oleg and hugged him.

"Oleg, you saved our lives!" she stammered.
"Well, I owed you my own life," said the Leopard simply.

Ivar, who had been alerted by all this noise, was hurrying back to his cave when he bumped into Fluster. Fluster started moaning pitifully. "I won't do it again, I promise! I'm sorry! I confess—it was me, but I'll never do it again!"

"Never do what again, crybaby?" roared Ivar, picking him up by the scruff of the neck.
"I led the hunters to your cave...it was because of that Leopard. I wanted...oh, don't squeeze me so tight...I only thought..."
"You little coward!" roared the furious Bear. "Well, this is the end of you!" And he was just about to crush the hare with his great paw when Oleg and Anoushka appeared on the scene.
"Let him go, Ivar," said the generous Leopard. "It's his nature; he can't help it."

Still growling with anger, Ivar flung the cowardly hare over his shoulder, and Fluster, only too happy to be let off so lightly, went away to hide in the woods.

However, Oleg knew that sooner or later the hunters would be back. If he stayed in the village his friends' lives would be in danger. He must go away again; he was fated to be on the run.

That evening he had a long conversation with Socrates. No one knew what it was about, except that something unusual was going to happen.

At dawn next day all the animals in the village went down to the beach. And suddenly they saw a surprising sight: Eugenia emerged slowly from the mist with...yes, with Oleg sitting on her blue back like a king on his throne! Socrates made a solemn speech from the top of his rock.

"Yes, my good people," he said, "you *can* believe your eyes. That *is* our friend Oleg the Snow Leopard on Eugenia's back. Eugenia persuaded me it was a good idea. There is a sunny country on the other side of the sea, a huge, fertile country where Oleg can live in peace, and Eugenia is taking him there. So let's all wish them a pleasant journey!"

Everyone cheered out loud. Anoushka, her eyes full of tears, blew Oleg a kiss with her paw, and Ivar roared as loud as he could, while the cubs, who did not understand what was going on, tumbled happily about. As Oleg and Eugenia left the bay, Oleg looked up at the castle balcony. Cosily wrapped in a pink woolly shawl, a little creature stood there, graciously bowing her elegant white head: Oleg recognized Guinevere, who had come to see her big cousin off.

Then the beach of black sand vanished into the mist. Eugenia, looking radiantly happy, gathered speed and made for the open sea with the beautiful Leopard on her back. They were going away together; her dream had come true!